Treasures
at the Museum

By Deborra Richardson

Illustrations by George Hilton III

Treasures at the Museum

Published by
The Elevator Group
Paoli, Pennsylvania

Copyright © 2011 by Deborra Richardson

Library of Congress Control Number: 2010927181

Trade Paperback: ISBN 978 0 9824945 1 6

Illustrations by George Hilton III
Jacket and interior design by Stephanie Vance-Patience

Published in the United States by The Elevator Group.

This book was printed in the United States.

To order additional copies of this book, contact:
The Elevator Group
45 Darby Road, Suite E-2
Paoli, PA 19301
www.TheElevatorGroup.com
610-296-4966 (p) • 610-644-4436 (f)
info@TheElevatorGroup.com

Dedication

*To Donovan, Savannah, Gabrielle,
and Jacqueline, who inspired me to write this book,
and to My Ka, Angel, and Jordan, who have
inspired me to write the next one.*

Acknowledgment

This book was born of a desire to reach the children in my life and to share with them the work that my colleagues and I do. I wanted to teach children about the treasures that could be found in archives, libraries, and museums. As I put this book together, I received help from librarians, such as Eboni Cole; teachers, such as Myrtle Harris; friends in book circles, such as Rosalye Settles; student assistants, such as Kristen Rohde, Christine Friis, and Kianna Duncan; and my god-daughter, Michele Stanback.

Special thanks for getting me started go to my librarian friend and colleague, Sharon Green, and to my publisher, Sheilah D. Vance, Esq. I would not have reached this place without either. For their ongoing love and sustenance I thank Alex and Jackie Richardson. And for keeping me motivated, I thank my husband, Bruce Pippinger; our families who gave us nieces, nephews, and grandchildren; and especially, my parents, Agnes and Ernest Boyd, whose continued support gave me the impetus always to find the best of myself.

—Deborra Richardson

Discovery

"Hooray for Saturday! Aunt Imani's coming to get us! We're going to the museum."

"Mom, do we have to?" fussed Robbie. "We're not even going to the museum. Aunt Imani said we're going to look at the archives there. Who cares about some moldy old stuff anyway?"

Just then, Aunt Imani came to the door.

"Hi kids," she said, giving each of them a hug. "Are you ready to go?"

Robbie resisted his aunt's hug. He walked over to the couch, plopped himself down, folded his arms across his chest, and pulled his face into a pout.

"Robbie, what's the matter with you?"

Aunt Imani was met with silence.

"He said he didn't want to go to some moldy old

archives," whispered Brittany. "What are archives?"

"This one is the place where Maxi works," said Aunt Imani.

Robbie heard Maxi's name and pretended that he was not interested. They always had fun when Maxi and Aunt Imani took them places. Maybe this would be fun, too. But he stayed on the couch with his arms folded. His face wasn't quite as pouty, though.

"Robbie, do you remember the pictures of you and Brittany that your Mom brings out when the folks get together?" asked Aunt-Tee. The children called her that for short, especially when they were tired or in a hurry.

"Yeah," Robbie said, grudgingly.

"What do you think they are?" Aunt-Tee asked.

"Just some dumb ol' pictures," mumbled Robbie.

"What happens when Mom or Dad brings them out?" Aunt-Tee asked.

"I know," said Brittany excitedly. "Sometimes we even bring out old projects we made and start telling stories!"

"That's right, those old pictures and crafts remind us of our pasts. They are OUR archives." Imani said.

"You mean Maxi works in a place where they tell stories?" Brittany asked. She was quite impressed.

"That's silly. Archives don't tell stories. I have archives," Robbie said importantly.

"You do? What are they?" asked Aunt-Tee, not quite believing that Robbie understood the word.

"Well… come on. I'll show you," Robbie said.

Robbie was getting excited. And though he wasn't sure that he wanted to show his private stash to his Aunt Imani, and certainly not to his little sister, he was surprised to realize he had archives of his own. Maybe this trip wouldn't be so bad after all.

The three left the house and went into the backyard.

"Wait here," Robbie said.

He went over to the big oak tree in the backyard and mounted the rungs to his tree house. It had come with the house when his parents bought it. Dad said that it was especially for him. No girls were allowed — and definitely not five year olds.

Besides, Brittany had her own private place in the attic.

Aunt Imani and Brittany could hear him banging things around inside.

Robbie moved a big box.

Then he moved a big bag.

Next he moved a pail and shovel.

There it was — his secret trunk. It was the size of an old steamer trunk, much like the one his Grandma took with her to college, only it looked like a cedar chest. He opened the lid and pulled out another box. Then he pulled

out a notebook and an envelope and mumbled to himself about what was left in the box.

He put the notebook and the envelope back in the box and set it aside. Then he closed the lid to the trunk. And he moved the pail and shovel, the big bag, and the big box back into place.

At eight, Robbie was no longer a little kid but he still did not feel he was quite big enough to handle the box and the climb from his tree house at the same time.

"Aunt-Tee, can you help me with this?" he called. There were no girls allowed anywhere near the tree house, but Aunt Imani was "all right."

Aunt Imani reached up for the box.

"Don't open it yet," Robbie said protectively.

Robbie came down from the tree house.

"What's in it?" Brittany wanted to know. Her

curiosity was making her impatient.

Again, Robbie opened the box and pulled out the notebook. It was full of his first and second grade writing assignments. Robbie thought it was silly, but his mother had asked him to keep them. She told him that they would make him smile one day. So, he kept them — hidden. As long as no one else could see them, he thought it might be okay. He didn't open the notebook for Aunt Imani and Brittany.

Next he pulled out the envelope again. It was manila, an office envelope, the kind Robbie saw in the principal's office or the nurse's office at school. It was big enough to keep letters and large pictures. In it were art projects, post cards from friends on summer vacation, and birthday cards from friends and family.

Robbie, Brittany and Aunt-Tee went back in the house to examine the treasures more closely. As they were thinking about them and remembering what each item meant, their Mom came in with a box of her own.

Mom's box contained the children's class pictures, their report cards, some family photos, and baby pictures, lots and lots of them.

"I remember that one," Brittany said, pointing to a particular snapshot. "Uncle Walter wanted to take our picture, and we wanted to swim in the baby pool. That was back when we were little. We kept throwing water on him, but he took the picture anyway."

"I would have liked to have seen that," laughed Aunt Imani. Uncle Walter was her brother. He was always teasing her and she enjoyed seeing him on the receiving end of the fun and jokes. "You do have archives, Robbie. Maxi takes care of objects like these at her job every day."

"Really? Like these?" Robbie asked, nodding his head in the direction of his treasures.

"Yes, just like these."

"Wow, can we go see her now? Maybe she can help me with mine," Robbie said.

"I'm ready when you are," Aunt Imani said. She looked at Robbie's smiling face, then at Brittany. She was smiling and excited.

"I'm ready," said Brittany.

"Let's go, kids."

The Trip

"Bye, Mom," they called as they tramped back through the house and out the front door. They got into the car and pulled out of the driveway.

Aunt Imani was a good driver and a great tour guide.

On the way, they passed the Basilica of the National Shrine of the Immaculate

Conception with the big colorful dome.

"That's beautiful," Brittany said with awe. "Can we stop here?"

"Not today, but we'll put that on our list of sites to see in DC. We'll come back soon," promised Aunt-Tee.

Next they passed the main post office on Massachusetts Avenue.

"There's a museum here, too," shared Aunt-Tee.

"I collect stamps. Can you see a lot of stamps here?" Robbie asked.

"Yes, you can, and there are all sorts of stories on display about moving the mail. You can see old planes, horses, and even stagecoaches in the exhibits," said Aunt Imani.

They passed the U.S. Capitol and two other museums while Aunt Imani was talking about the Postal Museum.

Then, "Look at that! What is it?" exclaimed Brittany.

It must have been at least twenty or twenty five feet tall, as tall as a house. It was royal blue on top. The royal blue part looked like spider legs. Around the middle, there was a silver band holding the spider legs together. On the bottom was a huge pink wheel with a shiny flat disk attached at the center.

"Oh, that's a giant ink eraser, the kind that Maxi and I used when we were in school. It's one of the art works in the National Gallery of Art's sculpture garden. There are other sculpture gardens at the Smithsonian. Each of them has several pieces of outdoor art," shared Aunt Imani.

"Man, we gotta come back here and maybe see the other gardens, too," Robbie said. He was thrilled by the sights as they passed them by.

15

"I'll make a note of this one, too." Aunt-Tee assured them.

Brittany and Robbie were so captivated by the sculpture garden that Aunt-Tee forgot to mention the National Archives and the Smithsonian National Museum of Natural History.

Finally, they began to look for a parking space. It took them a while, but they did find one on the National Mall, not too far from the Smithsonian National Museum of American History.

The Visit

They walked across Madison Drive, across the sidewalk, and up the shallow marble steps to a gigantic rectangular building.

There was a steel and black marble sculpture out front. And there was writing on the walls of the building.

"What's it say?" asked Brittany.

"I don't know, and I can't read it in this bright sunlight. Let's go inside. Maybe they can tell us at the information desk," said Aunt Imani.

But when they got inside, there was so much to see, they forgot to ask.

First, they stopped at the colossal screen that showed object after object they might see on display. Brittany and Robbie were fascinated by the number and variety of things that passed before them. They wanted to see everything.

"We came to see Maxi today," reminded Aunt-Tee. "Each of you can choose an exhibit. We'll spend some time at each of your choices, and then we'll find Maxi. She can tell us about the archives,

and maybe she'll join us for lunch."

"Brittany, what would you like to see?"

"Can we stop at the Lunch Counter?" asked Brittany.

"Okay, we'll stop at the Greensboro Lunch Counter. And Robbie?" asked Aunt Imani.

"I'd like to see the one on computers," said Robbie.

"That's on the first floor. The Greensboro Counter's up here. Let's start with that," said Aunt-Tee.

"Gee, sodas were only fifteen cents. That must have been ages ago. What's a 'sit-in'?" asked Brittany.

"It's a protest. A lot of people get together and sit in or in front of a business. They don't buy anything. They don't move, and they keep others from coming in. So the business loses money," explained Aunt Imani.

"Why would people do that?" asked Brittany.

"To make a point," Aunt Imani replied. "Remember Uncle Walter when he wanted to take your picture? He wouldn't let anything stop him, right?"

"Yeah."

"Well, he used that same feeling to work with the 1963 Mississippi Summer Project. That project got African American people registered to vote. The people who 'sat in' at the Greensboro Lunch Counter felt that we should have had the right to eat where we wanted. Uncle Walter and the people who 'sat in' were making a point. And they went to jail to make that point."

"Why did they go to jail?" asked Brittany.

"Back then, what they were doing was against the law. Uncle Walter helped to change that. You should be proud of him," said Aunt Imani.

Brittany was quiet for a while, thinking about what her Aunt had said, looking at herself in the mirror, and wondering how an African American girl like herself would have felt during those times. Brittany questioned whether she could have helped make things better, if she had lived then.

Robbie thought about it, too. He was proud, but he was also angry with what he had just heard.

Impatiently, he said, "Can we go to see the computers now?"

"Sure," said Aunt-Tee.

The three of them walked past the huge white

sculpture of George Washington, seated and wearing Greek-styled robes.

They got on the escalator, rode one flight down, and there they were.

"Awesome!" said Robbie.

"This is really neat!" said Brittany.

They were looking at the colorful animated stories on the screens above their heads. They saw Diana Ross and the Supremes, the disco dancing baby, and a short clip about tools working together without the benefit of human hands. After a few minutes of this, they went inside the exhibit. They quickly made their way past the inventions

of telegraph, telephone, phonograph, and radio. They stopped briefly to look at the old-fashioned televisions.

"That looks a little bit like the television we have in our kitchen," said Brittany. "Only it's bigger and heavier."

"I remember watching televisions that looked like that when I was about your age. Mom, Dad, Uncle Walter and I used to gather around it to watch 15-minute programs. They were in black and white back then."

"Did you have favorite shows?" asked Brittany.

"Yes I did," Aunt-Tee replied. "One of them was 'Diver Dan.' And Uncle Walter liked 'Clutch Cargo.'"

Robbie spotted the computers.

"Hey, over here!" he shouted.

Robbie was energetically designing his own dream bedroom. He had the mouse in hand. Point. Click. Point. Click. Point. Click.

For Robbie's room, he chose his favorite colors — purple and black, his favorite posters —Michael Jordan and Shaquille O'Neal, and his favorite

furniture — bunk beds.

"Aunt-Tee, come look at this!" he exclaimed.

"That's really lively, Robbie. I like that. Can we print it?"

They printed it out.

"My turn," said Brittany.

She chose her favorite soft tones of blue with the accents of hot pink, found soft cuddly dolls for her bed, and a really deep blue area rug.

"That's really nice," said Aunt-Tee. "It's getting late. Let's print it out and go find Maxi."

Lost

Robbie and Brittany were both tired and excited. Somehow, time spent with Aunt-Tee and Maxi always led to delightful and lively adventures.

Off they went with Aunt Imani as their pilot.

They walked to the left, to the right, up the escalator, down the stairs, and all around.

"This place is really big," Brittany observed. "We could get lost in here."

They rode the elevator. They walked the lobbies. They looked in exhibit halls. But they could not find Maxi.

"Where is Maxi, Aunt-Tee? I'm tired," whined Brittany.

They explored a little while longer. They traveled all over the building.

Finally, Robbie said, "Aunt-Tee, we'll never find Maxi's office this way."

"I know," wailed Brittany. "Where are we anyway? I don't remember this place. It's dark and spooky. And where are all the people?"

"Can we go back to the information desk?" suggested Robbie.

Before Aunt Imani could respond, a door opened. Light streamed out. And with it came a familiar sounding voice.

"Oh my goodness, what are you guys doing here?"

The Archives

It was Maxi. The trio had stumbled onto one of the back doors to the archives.

"Maxi! Girl, am I glad to see you!" said Aunt Imani. Brittany and Robbie ran to give Maxi a big hug. "Boy are we glad to see you!" they seconded.

"Their hearts are pounding like crazy, Imani. What's going on? Were you looking for the Archives Center?"

"Yes, Maxi. Actually we were looking for you." Aunt Imani said. "We couldn't find you anywhere. You found us instead!"

Maxi smiled. "Come on, I'll lead you to the front

door. I was slipping out the back way."

"Ooh, you work here?" asked Brittany, excitedly, her eyes wide as she looked around the large research room.

"Is this your archives?" Robbie wanted to know.

"Yes, Honey," Maxi replied.

"I brought my special archives with me. Can you help me with it?" Robbie wondered.

"Maybe. What do you want to do with it?" asked Maxi.

"I don't know — maybe help it tell a story? Are there exhibits here?" Robbie asked.

Maxi answered, "We have small exhibits outside and collections inside."

"What kinds of collections?" asked Brittany.

"Well, we collect paper materials, like diaries, appointment books, shopping receipts, concert programs and other similar items that come with the objects that you see on display," explained Maxi.

"How do they tell a story?" asked Robbie.

"Well," said Maxi, "I think the best way to understand how archival materials tell stories is to look at our displays outside the front door. Afterwards, since it is near closing, I'll be glad to show you around."

Brittany and Robbie oohed and aahed over the display cases.

They saw pictures,

press releases (short articles announcing upcoming events),

magazine ads,

and newspaper articles.

This was a display of Famous Amos memorabilia. Now they were really enthusiastic about finding out more. They reminded Maxi of her promise to show them around the inside of the Archives Center, behind the scenes.

"We have several hundred collections here," said Maxi. "The Famous Amos collection tells a story about American businessmen and women and their creativity. It gives us a peek into the history of advertising and business ownership in the United States."

"We also have collections that show us the

history of technology and American music," she added.

"We know about American music," said Robbie, jumping into the latest dance step.

"And technology. Would that be about computers and web sites?" Brittany asked. "We just came from the Information Age exhibit. Do you have collections that connect to it?"

"Yes, like the kinds of technology that happened in American businesses and homes before the computer.

The telegraph.

The light bulb.

Radio.

And television, for examples," said Maxi.

Pointing to a storage box, Robbie asked, "What's this, Maxi?"

"That's a special kind of box we use to protect the materials," said Maxi.

"Would this help keep my stuff safe, too?" asked Robbie.

"It would for a time, Sweetie. Did you say you brought your collection with you?"

Robbie nodded.

"Let's work with a few of your materials. And Robbie, I'm doing this because you and Brittany are special. The Chief rarely allows young people in the archives. So this is a special privilege."

They looked through Robbie's pictures and cards and chose a few. Maxi pulled out a special see-through envelope she called a mylar sleeve and gave it to Robbie. She showed Robbie and Brittany how to put things in the sleeves.

Robbie put two pictures in the sleeve, back to back.

Then Maxi gave a sleeve to Brittany. She only put one card in the sleeve so you could read what was written on the back.

"Wow!" said Brittany. "Is this all it takes?"

"We also use acid-free folders and boxes like the one you pointed out, Robbie."

"What's acid-free mean?" Brittany asked.

"Well… mylar sleeves, and acid-free folders and boxes are made in a special way to help protect valuable, historical materials."

"This is great, Maxi. Now I can take care of my stuff!" exclaimed Robbie.

"Maxi, you have so many boxes. How do you find what you're looking for?" Brittany asked.

"We describe the collection in a little booklet called a finding aid. And we give each collection a number. The collections are listed by number in a locator guide. We use the guide to find the collections on the shelves." Maxi pointed to the three-ringed binders that housed the locator guide.

"Wow! Can we try to find a collection with these?" asked Brittany.

"Sure, let's see. Remember Famous Amos?" asked Maxi.

"Chocolate chip cookies. My favorite!" exclaimed Robbie.

"That's right. Let's look for his collection."

"Let's hurry! Now I'm ready to eat!" said Robbie.

After finding the Famous Amos collection on the shelves, Brittany and Robbie were ready to go.

"Let's go kids," said Aunt-Tee. "Will you join us, Maxi?"

"Sure. Let's go," said Maxi.

And off they went to the Ice Cream Parlor for chocolate chip desserts.

More Fun Activities
and Information

Let's Talk About It 45

A Brief (and non-boring) History
   of the Smithsonian Institution
   and Its Archives 49

Activities. 53

What Do These Words Mean? 56

43

Let's Talk About It

- Have you ever visited any of the Smithsonian museums in Washington, DC? If so, which was your favorite, and why?

- Have you ever been to the archives at a museum? If so, what did you like the best? What do you still have questions about?

- Do you have your own special collection? If so, what do you collect? How long have you been collecting? Do you keep it in a special place?

- Is there something you'd like to start collecting? What is it, and why is it interesting to you?

- What other kinds of collections do you think you could find besides Famous Amos in the Archives Center at the Smithsonian's National Museum of American History? What other American businesses can you name, and do you think they also have archival collections?

- Do you think it was right of Robbie to hide his archives chest from his family in his tree house? Why or why not?

- Do you have someone special in your life that you love having adventures with? Who is it? Where have you been? What special memories do you have of your visit? Draw a picture and give a short summary of the visit.

- Our brains hold memories, which are really like archives if you think about it! Can you think of a place that you've visited and can you describe the place in detail just by thinking about it in your mind? Where was it? Why do you remember it? Did you like it? Write a story about it, and be sure to include a beginning, middle and end.

- If you could compare Robbie and his sister Brittany, what could you say about them? What kind of room did Robbie create on the computer? What were some of the special things Brittany wanted in the room that she designed? If you were able to design your perfect room, what would it look like?

A Brief (and non-boring) History of the Smithsonian Institution and its Archives

The Smithsonian Institution was founded in 1846 and is named after James Smithson, a British scientist who left his collection to the United States Government. He wanted to create a scientific research center that everyone could use. It is very interesting to note that James Smithson never even made a visit to the United States! As time went

James Smithson

by, more donors (people who give their treasures away) gave items to the Smithsonian for everyone to enjoy. The museum grew large enough so that many different groups of people and areas of study were included. Today, there are nineteen facilities including museums, research centers and a zoo that make up the Smithsonian Institution. Most of the buildings are located on the National Mall between the United States Capitol building and the very tall Washington Monument—better known as the "needle–looking" tower. The Smithsonian includes the National Museum of Natural History (dedicated to topics such as dinosaurs, evolution, gems and marine life), the National Museum of American History (which showcases people such as Martin Luther King, Jr., Abraham Lincoln, and even Mary Pickerskill, the woman who stitched the flag that inspired the U.S. National Anthem),

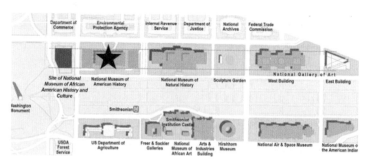

the National Air and Space Museum, the National Museum of African Art, and the National Museum of the American Indian, to name a few!

Today, the Smithsonian Institution has more than a dozen units that take care of archives and special collections. Along with the National Archives and Records Administration and the Library of Congress, all in Washington, DC, these three institutions hold the country's largest collections of archival materials.

Activities

Make your own Archives Tool Kit!!

Recycle a shoe box and let it house your treasures, just like Robbie did! You can decorate your box with construction paper, photographs (make sure to OK that with the grown-ups if there is only one copy of the photo), ribbons, magazine cut-outs—anything really!

Once you are finished, go to your local school supply store or grocery store and get some plastic sleeves which are great for making sure any photographs, drawings, or hand-written papers stay in tip-top shape—just like in the book!! What will you put in your archive?

Critical Thinking

- The book talks about Robbie and Brittany's visit to the Smithsonian's National Museum of American History. What kind of archives do you think might be held there? Remember how Maxi had the children search for the cookie maker Famous Amos? Make a list of things that you think might be included in the museum's very large collection and compare it with your classmates. How many of you had similar items on your lists?

- Next—why do you think museums collect things and place them in archives? Why might it be important to save things if they are old? What kind of people do you think might use the archives?

A Visit to the Museum

Plan a visit to your local museum or even the

Smithsonian's National Museum of American History. After visiting the museum, tell us what exhibit was your favorite and why? Draw a picture that describes the favorite part of your visit and write a brief summary about it. Did anyone else pick the same exhibit? What other exhibits did your friends or classmates choose? Share your stories with each other!! Have your teacher make them into a book that showcases your fun experience!

Interview Someone — And Record it!

Interviewing someone older than you can help uncover a great deal of information about the past. Choose from a family member, friend or teacher and ask them questions such as: where were you born? What was your favorite toy growing up? When do you remember using your first computer? What was your favorite vacation? You can either write down your interview answers or record them on a tape recorder or digital recorder to capture your voices!

What Do These Words Mean?

Archives: A collection or collections of important historical items such as letters, books, photographs, and audio clips.

Basilica of the National Shrine of the Immaculate Conception: One of the ten largest churches in the world, located in Washington, DC. It has a beautiful blue and gold circular dome on the top of the main building and one tall and pointy bell tower.

Stagecoach: A horse-drawn carriage that carried mail throughout the United States in the old days.

Steel: A silver colored metal used to make buildings strong and give them support.

Marble: A type of stone used for many buildings and statues. It can be colorful, white or black, and it is often shiny and cold to the touch.

George Washington: He was the first President of the United States from 1789-1797.

Colossal: A word used to describe something that is very large.

Telegraph: A machine used for communicating before the invention of the telephone. You couldn't hear the other person's voice on the other end, instead, you would use a series of codes sent over a wire that represented words.

Phonograph: An old record player invented shortly before 1900. The sound would come out of a large tuba-shaped horn.

Lobby: Another name for a waiting room or the area where you enter a building.

Collection: A bunch of objects gathered for study that usually have similar traits in common. You can also collect similar things like stickers, stamps or baseball cards. When you group them together, that is called a collection.

Exhibit: To show an important collection for all to enjoy. Museums set up exhibits and set aside special areas so that many people can learn about a specific time or culture.

Materials: The things or items you are collecting.